© Creation, script and illustrations:
A. M. Lefèvre, M. Loiseaux, M. Nathan-Deiller, A. Van Gool.
First published and produced by
Creations for Children International, Belgium.
www.c4ci.com
This English edition published by
Peter Haddock Publishing, United Kingdom, YO16 6BT.
All rights reserved.
Printed in China.

Peter and
the Wolf

illustrated by Van Gool

One cold day
Peter went for a walk.
A bird flew with him.
It was his friend.
They met a duck.
"Hello, Duck,"
they said.

The bird flew to the ground.
A cat jumped
at the bird.
"Watch out!"
cried Peter.
The cat missed.
The bird flew up
into the tree.

"Peter,
go back inside,"
said Grandad.
"The wolf is around."
Peter was sad.

The wolf was near.
He saw the duck.
He jumped
at the duck,
and ate it!

Peter was still inside.
He wanted to be outside.
He looked through the fence.

The bird and
the cat sat
on a branch
of a tree.

Peter had to help them.
He got a rope.

He climbed up the tree
to the cat
and the bird.
"Fly at the wolf,"
said Peter to the bird.

"Tease him,
but be careful."
The wolf was angry.
But he could not catch
the bird.
Peter made a big knot
in the rope.

He threw the rope around
the wolf's tail.
Peter pulled hard.
The wolf
was captured.
The cat and the bird
were saved.

Some hunters came by.
They were looking for the wolf.

They saw Peter
in the tree.
The wolf was trapped
in the tree.

Grandad came by.
Peter and Grandad were happy.
"I caught the wolf,
Grandad!"

Grandad was proud
of Peter.
Peter was happy.
He led the way
back home singing.

Pinocchio

illustrated by Van Gool

Geppetto carved
models from wood.
One day he made
a little wooden boy.

"I wish
he were real
and could live
with me,"
he said.

Then the little wooden boy
came alive!

"I will call you Pinocchio,"
he said.
He gave him books
and
sent him to school.

On the way,
Pinocchio joined a puppet show.
He danced so well
he was given five gold coins.
"Geppetto will be pleased,"
he thought.

But then he met two crooks.
They all went to an inn for
a meal and a bed for the night.

When Pinocchio went to sleep
he dreamed of being rich.

Next day
the crooks showed him
a place to bury his gold coins.

"They will grow into
a money tree,"
they said.
Pinocchio waited patiently.

Of course,
the crooks stole his money
while he slept.

Afraid to go home,
he saw a woman with blue hair.
He begged her to help him.
She was a fairy.

When Pinocchio told lies
his nose began to grow long.
"Go home to your father
and be good,"
the fairy said.
Then his nose
grew normal again.

On the way home,
Pinocchio stopped at Funland.
He could eat
free ice-creams all day!

He didn't know
they would change him
into a donkey.

Pinocchio was sold to a circus.
He was treated so badly
that soon he couldn't walk.

"Throw him into the sea,"
ordered the circusmaster.

The sea changed him back
into a wooden boy.

A huge whale swallowed him.

Inside the whale was Geppetto,
who had been looking for him.

"Climb on my back,"
said a big fish,
that was also there.
"I will take you home."

At home,
Pinocchio looked after Geppetto
with great care.

"You are a good boy now,"
said the blue fairy.
She turned Pinocchio
into a real boy.

At last Geppetto had a proper son!